Henry V

Written by William Shakespeare

Retold by J.A. Henderson

Illustrated by Giorgio Bacchin

Collins

Characters

King Henry V of England

King Charles VI of France

The dauphin: the son of King Charles VI of France

Bishop of Ely: a friend of the Archbishop of Canterbury

Archbishop of Canterbury: the most important bishop in England

Duke of Exeter:
one of Henry's loyal
friends and advisers

**Duke of
Westmoreland:**
one of Henry's loyal
friends and advisers

Mistress Quickly:
Pistol's wife

Bardolph: an old
friend of Henry's

Pistol: an old friend
of Henry's

Nym: an old friend
of Henry's

Scroop:
a traitor

Grey:
a traitor

Cambridge:
a traitor

Prologue

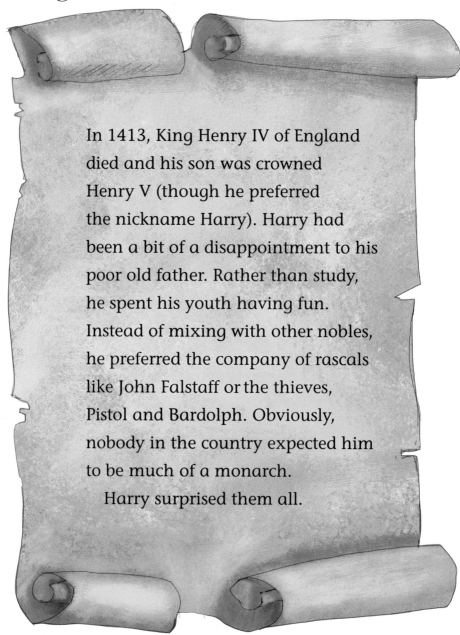

In 1413, King Henry IV of England died and his son was crowned Henry V (though he preferred the nickname Harry). Harry had been a bit of a disappointment to his poor old father. Rather than study, he spent his youth having fun. Instead of mixing with other nobles, he preferred the company of rascals like John Falstaff or the thieves, Pistol and Bardolph. Obviously, nobody in the country expected him to be much of a monarch.

Harry surprised them all.

Chapter 1

In a shadowy corner of his abbey, the Archbishop
of Canterbury was plotting with the Bishop of Ely.
"Parliament's thinking about taking a lot of lands
that belong to the church and using the money they
bring in to help the poor." The archbishop fiddled
with the solid gold rings on his fingers, horrified by
the idea. "We need King Henry to stop it, or we're
going to lose a fortune!"

"Do you think he'll help us?" the bishop whispered. "He's changed, after all. Given up his wild ways and even his old friends. He seems determined to be fair and just these days." The bishop didn't sound sure if this was a good thing. "He might not agree to help us keep our lands."

"Oh, I think I can convince him," the archbishop smirked. "You know he has his eye on the riches of France, don't you?"

The bishop did indeed. Henry's great grandfather, Edward III, had once ruled both England and France. Those French lands were lost now but the young king felt they should still belong to his family. It was no secret, he wanted them back.

"I'll persuade him to invade and take what's rightfully his. In fact, I'll even give him the money to raise an army." The archbishop smiled slyly. "So long as he stops Parliament from grabbing our money."

Chapter 2

A few days later, hunched forwards on the throne, Henry faced the Archbishop of Canterbury. On either side sat the king's advisers, the noblemen Exeter and Westmoreland. Despite being much younger than them, Henry seemed confident and relaxed, looking every inch a monarch.

"You say my claim to rule France is a fair one." He beckoned the archbishop closer. "Yet two great nations never go to war without a lot of bloodshed, so be very careful you're being honest about it."

Canterbury swallowed hard. Suddenly, he was a lot less sure about his plan. But it was too late to back down. "I've looked into every legal argument I can find on the subject, sire," he replied, opening a huge book of notes. "And here they are."

The archbishop reeled off an endless list of boring facts and figures. After five minutes, Exeter's head began to droop and Westmoreland gave a loud yawn. Finally, the archbishop finished his long-winded argument and bowed.

Henry was staring at him coldly.

"Just a simple answer will do," he said slowly and menacingly. "Am I, or am I NOT entitled to the lands of France?"

"Yes." The archbishop wiped sweat from his brow. "Definitely."

"And you'll take them!" Exeter and Westmoreland leapt to their feet, always eager for action. "With us fighting by your side!"

But Henry was no longer a rash youth and still wasn't convinced. "What about those sneaky Scots in the north?" he asked. "You know what they're like."

He had a point. Every time an English king took off to fight in foreign lands, the Scots saw an opportunity for a bit of raiding across the border.

"Then only take a quarter of your army to France," Canterbury suggested. "The rest can stay here and defend England."

Exeter and Westmoreland glared at him. They were the military brains, not some weedy archbishop who'd never lifted a sword. Using a fraction of England's army against a mighty nation like France didn't seem like much of a plan. Before they could voice any doubts, however, Henry spoke.

"Send in the French ambassadors and we'll see what they have to say."

The ambassadors had been sent by the dauphin, the proud and arrogant son of the French king. Henry was surprised to see they were carrying a wooden chest.

"My master, the dauphin, has sent you this," the lead ambassador said uneasily. "He thinks it'd be a better prize for someone of your age and inexperience than his lands, which you falsely claim."

The king raised an eyebrow. Perhaps the dauphin was offering him riches as a bribe to prevent the coming fight. The chest was a bit small, though. He nodded for Exeter to look inside.

"Treasure?" Henry asked hopefully.

Exeter flipped open the lid. "Eh … No. Tennis balls."

"My master says you've no chance of winning against him." The messenger winced. "So … eh … you may as well stay where you are and play tennis."

Henry went red at the insult. The dauphin obviously thought he was no real threat. Well, he'd show that jumped-up brat. He fought his temper down and gave the terrified ambassador his most pleasant smile.

"So your master thinks I should still be playing games, rather than ruling a kingdom?"

The ambassador knew better than to answer.

"Then tell him this is one game he won't enjoy. Because this little prank will cause castles to fall and thousands of his men to die. When we play, I won't be using tennis balls. I'll be using cannonballs. And the prize for my victory will be his father's throne."

He dismissed the messengers with a sneer. "We'll see who's laughing at his silly joke then, shall we?"

"You certainly told them, sire," Exeter said proudly, as the ambassadors slunk off. "I'll start raising an army and preparing our navy to set sail."

Chapter 3

Word of Henry's invasion plan spread throughout the land, and ordinary folk rushed to take part. Even his old friends, Bardolph, Pistol and Nym, felt they should join in. They missed the old days, laughing and partying with wild young Harry, but understood why they were over. Henry needed to act like a sensible and respectable king now, and his former friends couldn't seem to stop getting into trouble, even with each other.

Bardolph, Pistol and Nym met at Nell Quickly's inn, where they'd spent so many merry nights with the prince. It only brought back sad memories now he wasn't around. Nym was in a particularly bad mood. Nell Quickly had been his fiancée but had gone and married Pistol instead. Nym was looking for a fight before the war with the French had even started.

"Run off with my old lady, would you?" He drew his sword when Pistol appeared. "I've a good mind to cut you down to size."

"You're welcome to try." Pistol grabbed his own weapon. "I'll soon show you who's the better man."

"Cut it out, you two." Bardolph got between them. "Or I'll kill you both myself, before the French get a chance." He pushed them roughly apart. "C'mon. Weren't we all pals once?"

Bardolph sighed loudly. Harry had held them together with his good spirits, and Bardolph missed him. They all did. Harry's best friend, old John Falstaff, had suffered the most. He'd taken it very badly when the king seemed to reject his friendship, and had recently died. Of a broken heart, Bardolph suspected.

There was nothing to be done. If Henry hadn't parted company with his friends, people would never have stopped gossiping about it.

He's still hanging out with the lowest of the low, they'd whisper. He's not fit to rule his own country, never mind France.

Bardolph didn't like to think of himself as the lowest of the low. It hurt. But he was a thief, there was no denying it. Harry needed to place the welfare of his country over the feelings of his old mates. Bardolph, Pistol and Nym would follow their king into battle anyway. The trio were still loyal to him. It was how the world worked.

"Shall we go, Pistol?" Bardolph headed for the door. "It's a long walk to Southampton where the ships leave."

"Goodbye, my love." Mistress Quickly kissed Pistol, and Bardolph gave her a peck on the cheek, too. Nym made to do the same, until Pistol glared at him.

"Best not, eh?" Nym backed away. "Let's head off, lads."

Chapter 4

Meanwhile, the French were getting ready for war and saw no reason to play fair. Instead of waiting for Henry to sail across the channel, why not get rid of this noisy upstart before he even arrived on their shores? It would save a lot of lives, after all. So the French asked three English noblemen to help them – Scroop, Grey and Cambridge.

The French plan was simple. Offer these men riches, if they'd kill their king.

Henry was clever, however, and had no intention of going to war without finding out more about his enemy. He'd employed many spies of his own, and it didn't take them long to discover the plans to kill him.

Henry believed in acting with honour, and had hoped the French thought the same way. It saddened him that they'd try something so deceitful. Wars had rules, after all, and kings and nobles were supposed to act with decency.

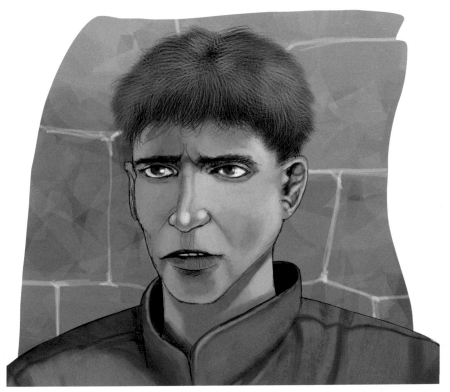

But if the dauphin's actions disappointed Henry, the treachery of Scroop, Grey and Cambridge filled him with fury. Henry was their rightful king, and only men without a shred of pride would betray their ruler for money. He considered having them taken away in the middle of the night and disposed of. If they wanted to creep around in the shadows, then they could die there.

But no. People like that should be exposed, Henry decided. Partly as a warning to others, and partly to show how two-faced traitors were.

He decided to set a test that would show their true colours to everyone. So he summoned all the nobles to a war council, including Scroop, Grey and Cambridge.

The commanders stood round a large table, looking at the invasion plans. Scroop, Grey and Cambridge were amongst them.

"We're almost ready," Henry said. Then he paused, as if remembering something. "Oh, by the way, we arrested some fellow yesterday. He was saying all sorts of awful stuff about me. Talking treason. That kind of thing."

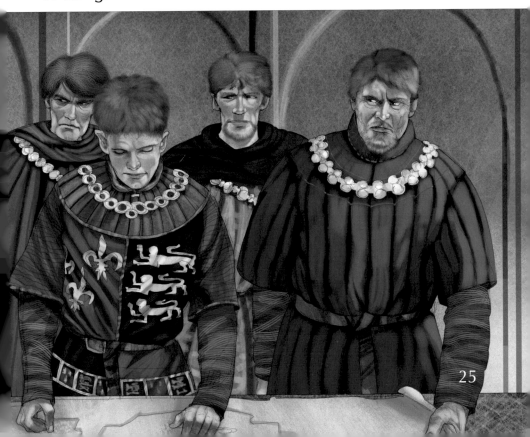

He looked calmly at the conspirators. "What do you think I should do?"

"Behead him, of course," Scroop replied, without hesitation.

"I don't think he meant any real harm," the king objected.

"Still, you have to punish him, my lord," Cambridge joined in. "To set an example."

"Really?" Henry put on an innocent look. "He was probably just bragging to sound important. I was actually going to let him go."

"Show no mercy, sire." Grey placed a hand on Henry's shoulder. "If you pardon one person who starts plotting against you, more will do the same."

"How very true." Henry stepped away from them, his eyes blazing. "Exeter? Westmoreland? Arrest these three villains."

The conspirators turned pale. Grey's hand went to his sword, but he was too late. Exeter pinned him to the wall and Westmoreland's guards overpowered Cambridge and Scroop.

"I'll take your advice, gentlemen." Henry's voice had turned cold and flat. "As you were so quick to insist, traitors must be shown no mercy. Especially those who'd sell out their king and country for a bag of silver."

He shook his head sadly. "Thankfully I still have some loyal men, and they told me what you were plotting. Did you really think you could get away with this?" He beckoned to Exeter and Westmoreland. "Take these monsters away and cut their heads off."

Chapter 5

The dauphin was still convinced Henry would be easy to beat, but his father, the King of France, wasn't so sure. He was worried by Henry's determination and the admiration he inspired in his people. In a last attempt to avoid war, he finally offered Henry a small part of France called Aquitaine and the hand in marriage of his daughter, Katharine.

Though Henry'd taken quite a fancy to Princess Katharine, the French king's offer was too little, too late.

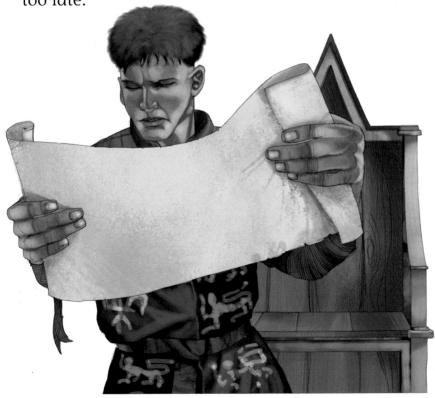

In April 1415, Henry's fleet landed in northern France and attacked the town of Harfleur, where part of the French army was based. The English army managed to break down one wall, but when they tried to force their way into the town, the French fought back fiercely.

Night after night, Henry's men tried to break through, only to be forced back by the town's defenders. Arrows rained down on the troops. Boiling oil was poured over them from the ruined walls. Cannonballs tore apart the ranks of advancing English soldiers. Faced with such ferocious fighting, the invaders seemed destined to fail. It looked as if the dauphin was right. Henry was stumbling at the first hurdle.

However, King Henry wasn't one to give up.
Seeing his men struggling, he rode through flames,
dust and flying arrows, urging them forwards. "Once
more into the breach, my friends!" he cried, rearing up
on his horse. "Bare your teeth. Raise yourself to your
full height and show the enemy what you're made of!"

Outlined against the fiery sky, his eyes glittered in the darkness. "Follow my lead and, upon this charge, fight for Harry, England and St George!" Henry galloped towards the town and his troops rushed forwards with him, screaming fearsome war cries.

"Yeah! Show them how we English fight!" Bardolph, Pistol and Nym shouted encouragement from safely at the back. "We'll be along in a minute." They turned and headed in the opposite direction.

"I think we've done our bit," Pistol said. "Let's go and hide in those bushes till it's all over."

"Get fighting, you three." A passing captain urged them forwards, using the point of his sword. "Or I'll be sticking my weapon in places you wouldn't like."

"We're going, Captain Sir," Pistol saluted. "No need to get personal!"

Despite his best efforts, Henry's army was still struggling to get past the remains of the town walls, so the king took a gamble. He rode right up to Harfleur's gates and pulled to a halt.

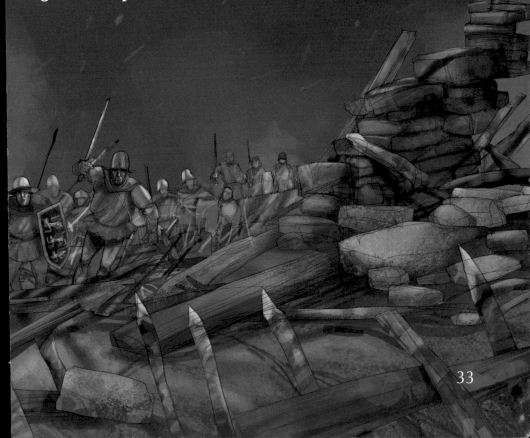

"Surrender now and you'll be treated fairly," he shouted to the town's French defenders. "You've my promise that any of our men caught looting will be put to death." He bit his lip and carried on. "If you don't surrender, however, the streets will run with blood. I'll burn this town to the ground and everyone in it. Your choice!"

One look at the shrieking mob behind Henry convinced the French that the warning was a serious one. With heavy hearts, they finally surrendered.

The king took Exeter aside. "They did as I asked," he said, with obvious relief. "Now we must show the French mercy, as I promised. Harm none of them. Not one person."

Exeter nodded grimly, deeply troubled. They'd won this battle, but at great cost. Many soldiers were dead or wounded and even more were sick. Worse, a huge French army was heading towards them. The French were too late to save Harfleur but, in this weakened state, the English wouldn't stand a chance against them.

Henry had no choice but to retreat. His army marched towards the port of Calais, intending to board their ships and set sail for another part of the coast. Once they'd rested, Henry thought, they could try again. But the French troops were fresh and strong and knew the country well. Henry knew they'd catch up before he reached his destination.

When the English finally halted, at a place called Agincourt, their enemy was right behind. That night, the two armies set up camp within shouting distance of each other. Henry's men were ill and exhausted. Yet, when dawn broke, there'd be a fight, no matter how badly he wanted to avoid it. Reluctantly, he gave orders to prepare for battle in the morning.

Chapter 6

As he watched the battle preparations, the king noticed a commotion in the distance and rode over. "What's going on here?" he demanded.

"We found this soldier stealing gold from a local church," the captain replied. "He'll be punished, of course. Apparently his name's Bardolph."

Henry went white. Bardolph. His old friend.

Yet he'd given his strongest oath that anyone caught looting should be executed – the king's orders. If the French were to be his people too, he had to treat them as fairly as the English. He must uphold his own law. "I stand by my word," he said eventually, tears in his eyes. "I can't let anyone off. Execute him."

Then he turned and galloped away, his mouth set in a grim line, leaving Bardolph to his fate.

That night, the miserable king couldn't sleep.
The French were so close he could hear them laughing
and see the twinkling lights of their camp fires.
Unlike Henry, they longed for morning, certain their
huge force would crush the tired, weak English army.

Henry got up and went out amongst his men, for
he needed to see if they still had the guts to fight.
He knew they'd put on a brave face for their king.
The only way to find out how they were really
feeling was if they thought he was simply another
common soldier.

He threw a cloak over his shoulders and turned
up the hood for disguise. Darkness would hide
his features.

Before long he came upon a group of men, deep
in conversation. He crept over.

"I'm not looking forward to tomorrow,"
one grumbled. "Don't much fancy our chances. I bet
the king wishes he was anywhere but here, too."

"I wish he was anywhere but here," another added.
"Then we wouldn't be in this mess."

"I'm sure the king's happy right where he is,"
said Henry, sitting down. He was careful to stay far
enough from the firelight, so they couldn't see his face.
"He's only doing his duty, after all."

"His duty?" The first soldier laughed bitterly. "He's the one who wanted this war. We're just following orders. What's more, he gets all the glory if we win." He spat on the ground. "But if we lose?" he continued. "Why, we'll die in the dirt, leaving widows and orphaned children. And it'll be his fault."

"Not that Harry'll care," his companion snorted. "The French will simply take him prisoner; then let him go when poor England pays enough ransom."

Henry gritted his teeth. "The king will never let himself be taken alive!" he retorted angrily. "He'll fight to the death, just like you."

"He's not like us." The soldier gave a bitter laugh. "We commoners mean nothing to him."

Henry got up and stormed away before he lost his temper. The man was wrong. Hadn't he been best friends with Pistol and Falstaff and Bardolph? Yet, the soldier had a point. He'd let Bardolph die, because he had to act like a king. The lives of every person here, and the fate of two entire nations, were in his hands. He couldn't afford to act or feel the way common men did, no matter how much he might wish it.

He knelt, wearily. "I've done my best to be a good person and a strong monarch," he muttered. "How can I make sure my troops have faith in me tomorrow, faced with such terrible odds? Because, if they don't, we won't survive." He thought about what the soldiers had said. That was the answer. He had to prove he was one of them.

And yet he'd never felt so alone.

Chapter 7

As the sun rose, so did the English army, but they were silent and gloomy. The men were worn out and afraid, and Henry's nobles weren't much happier.

"We're outnumbered five to one," Exeter muttered, "and the French aren't tired, like us."

"If only we had some more troops." Westmoreland sighed wearily. "I knew leaving most of the army back home was a bad idea."

"Why would you want more soldiers?" A hand landed on their shoulders and they spun round to see Henry standing behind them, a confident grin on his face. "If we're going to die, the less of us the better, eh? But if we win, the fewer men, the greater share of honour." He raised his voice so the troops could hear. "Still, if any of you want to leave, you're free to do so."

Many men looked tempted by the offer, but Henry wasn't finished.

"Think about this, though," he yelled. "Anyone who survives today can return home standing tall, for this battle is going down in history. It'll be remembered forever, and so will you, just for being here."

He rolled up his sleeve. "You can proudly show your friends and neighbours your scars. Tell your children how we few, we happy few, became a band of brothers."

He removed his crown and dropped it at the feet of the astonished crowd. "For anyone who fights with me today is my brother!"

His army struggled to their feet, shaking off all weariness. This wasn't the way a king talked! He was treating them as equals! Perhaps they stood a chance after all.

"When other men try to boast of great things they've achieved," Henry continued at the top of his lungs, "you can make them fall silent and bow their heads by simply saying these words."

He raised a gleaming sword in the air. "I fought alongside my king at Agincourt!"

The men roared and stamped their feet. The young monarch was right. Here was their one chance at true glory, before they went back to a hard dull life of working the fields.

"Still think we need more soldiers?" Henry winked at Westmoreland.

"I do not!" The general shook his head, caught up in the moment. "Why, you and I alone could take on the French!"

"Then let's get started!" Harry knew he'd won his army over. They'd fight like demons now.

If the enemy expected an easy victory, they were in for a terrible shock.

Chapter 8

At dawn, thousands of French soldiers on horseback charged across the fields towards the vastly outnumbered English. But Henry had chosen his position well. On either side were banks of trees, stopping the French horses spreading out.

The ground was marshy and the dauphin's mounted knights, in their heavy armour, were soon bogged down and moving slowly.

And King Henry had a secret weapon: 7,000 Welsh archers, armed with huge longbows. They drew and fired, drew and fired, until the sky turned black with feathered shafts.

Rank after rank of Frenchmen fell, and those behind couldn't get past their dead or wounded comrades. The few French knights who did reach the English ranks fared no better. The enemy were sheltering behind a barrier of pointed stakes, planted in the ground with the sharpened ends facing outwards. The French horses couldn't break through.

Seeing the battle was actually going in his favour, Henry urged his mount forwards. "Chaaaaarge!" he shouted. "It's now or never, lads!"

Henry's army poured between the gaps in the spikes and launched a furious attack against the bewildered French. Even Pistol and Nym joined in. The dauphin's once-proud army was in chaos, and those who could turned and fled.

The king sat in the mud with Exeter and Westmoreland, their armour dented and their faces covered with grime and blood. The field was littered with dead as far as the eye could see.

"We won!" Westmoreland was unable to hide his surprise. "The French have retreated. What's left of them, anyway."

"At what cost to my soldiers?" Henry said bleakly. "Tell me truthfully. How many died?"

"No, no. Most of our force are still alive, sire," Exeter grinned. "Our victory over the enemy was total. You're now king of France, and we can finally go home."

"They're no longer the enemy, good friend." The young king patted his companion on the knee. "If I were to think that way, all this slaughter would have been for nothing. No. The French are now my people too and I'll marry their Princess Katharine to prove it. I intend to rule my new people fairly and justly."

He looked up at the clear blue sky over Agincourt and smiled. "You might say I'm already home."

The Battle of Agincourt

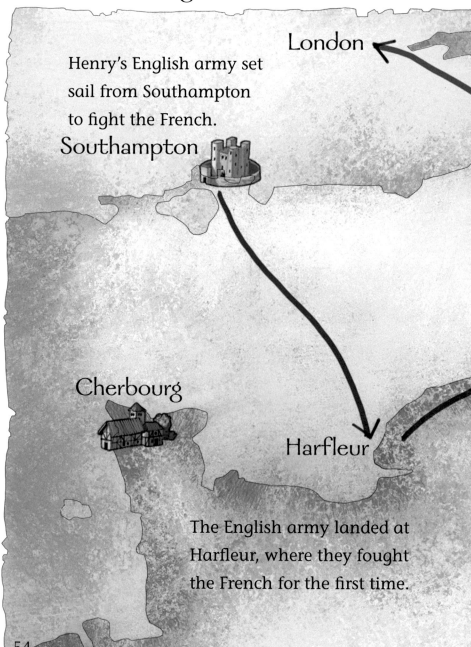

Henry's English army set
sail from Southampton
to fight the French.

Southampton

London

Cherbourg

Harfleur

The English army landed at
Harfleur, where they fought
the French for the first time.

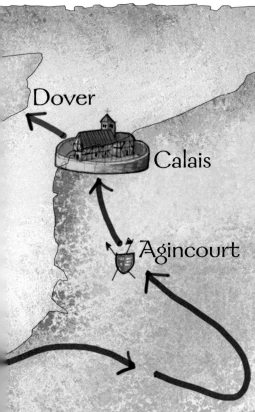

Dover

Calais

Agincourt

The English and French armies fought again at Agincourt near Calais. Although the English army was relatively small and weak, the English won. Henry was now ruler of France as well as England ... for a while at least.

After fighting at Harfleur, the English soldiers were exhausted and many were ill. Henry decided to head for Calais, but the French army was close behind.

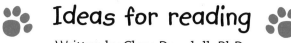

Ideas for reading

Written by Clare Dowdall, PhD
Lecturer and Primary Literacy Consultant

Reading objectives:
- check that the book makes sense to them, discussing their understanding and exploring the meaning of words in context
- draw inferences such as inferring characters' feelings, thoughts and motives from their actions, and justify inferences with evidence
- provide reasoned justifications for their views

Spoken language objectives:
- give well-structured descriptions, explanations and narratives for different purposes
- participate in discussions, presentations, performances, role play, improvisations and debates

Curriculum links: History – an aspect of British History; Geography – locational knowledge

Resources: map of France; ICT for research

Build a context for reading

- Ask children to suggest what qualities a good king (or queen) needs to possess.
- Look at the covers of the book. Read the blurb and discuss what challenges young Harry might have to deal with in the story.
- Explain that *Henry V* is one of Shakespeare's famous histories. Ask children to suggest when it might be set, and relate it to known periods in history, e.g. before Henry VIII.

Understand and apply reading strategies

- Turn to pp2–3. Read about each character and check that children understand each character's role and position in the kingdom (archbishop, duke, traitor).
- Read the prologue together. Check that children understand unfamiliar vocabulary. Remind them of strategies for understanding new vocabulary.